Ana in Dolly Land

Colleen E. Edwards

To order additional copies of this book, contact:
Xlibris
844-714-8691
www.Xlibris.com
Orders@Xlibris.com

ISBN: Softcover   978-1-6698-7326-6
       Hardcover   978-1-6698-7327-3
       EBook   978-1-6698-7325-9

Print information available on the last page

Rev. date: 04/05/2023

Dedication

In loving memory of my mother Ina Wilson, an only child who shared the stories of her life growing up as an only child. Her dolls were her imaginary sisters. She was raised by her mother Ella in Jamaica.

To those who are the only child in their families all over the world, whether you are an only child with no siblings or an only child due to an age difference, just remember you have a mommy and a daddy who loves you very much. You have little cousins and friends at school and church to play with. You are loved.

I am Ana. My dolls are beautiful, and I love playing with them. If I am in a sad mood, I bring my dolls out, and they cheer me up. I am an only child; my dolls are my sisters for now until I get a little sister. I will be seven years old in two months.

I love my dolls. Today, I am going to give them a bath and dress them up.

My dolls are Amanda, Krissy, and Melody. Amanda is tall and skinny. I am going to choose red as her favorite color. Krissy is short and medium-built. She will love to be in blue. My little Melody is so cute and small. I have chosen pink for her.

I am having a tea party today, and Amanda will do the planning. I have invited my other friends to bring their dolls to my tea party.

We will have sandwiches, cookies, milk, and juice at the party. My dolls will love this party. We plan to play games. As my friends arrive, I will give each of them balloons of different colors.

After the tea party today, I will plan a sing-along with my friends and my dolls. We had a sing-along before, and it was so much fun—we sang and sang and sang.

Mom plans to take me shopping tomorrow. When we go to the store, I will look around for new clothes and little toys for my dolls.

I have been asking mom to allow my friends to sleep over. Mom said she is still thinking about it. If we have a sleepover, I will invite my friends to bring their dolls to the sleepover. My friend Kim has three dolls, and she is getting another one on her birthday. I would like another doll, but mom says I already have enough.

One day, I cannot find Amanda. I search under the bed, in my closet, in the living room, and in my toy box. I go into a panic. Mom helps me search. We find Amanda under the sofa in the living room.

Our dog, Busta, was playing with Amanda under the sofa. Mom gives Busta a warning about moving the doll.

Melody needs a lot of care; she is so small. I feed her and put her to bed most of the time. She is the baby and needs her sleep. Amanda would like to play with Melody all day, I don't allow it, though. Melody needs to sleep.

I make up a song, and I sing it to my dolls. Do you want to hear it? It goes: I love my dolls. I love my dolls. I love my dolls, my beautiful dolls. My dolls are cute. My dolls are pretty. I love my dolls. Do you like my song, Busta? I love my dolls.

I wish I could take my dolls to school. The teacher says we are not allowed to bring dolls into the classroom. At school, though, I have other children to play with. My friends who have sisters and brothers talk about them. I talk about my dolls.

When I talk about my dolls, I feel happy. I wish I could have my dolls with me at all times. Since I cannot take my dolls to school, we have school when I get home.

I teach my dolls the alphabet—A, B, C, D, E, F, G, and so on. I also teach them to count—1, 2, 3, 4, 5, 6, 7, 8 9, and 10. Amanda *is* catching on really fast; she is a fast learner. I have to spend more time with Krissy and little Melody, but they are catching on as well. I read to my dolls. They listen and fall asleep while I am reading.

I also teach them prayers—God is good, God is great. Mom says one of these days, I will have a brother or sister to play with. For now, all I have are my dolls. I love my dolls, though. I love my dolls. I love my dolls. My dolls are pretty. My dolls are sweet. I love my dolls.

Printed in the United States
by Baker & Taylor Publisher Services